**Lisa Greathouse**

**Assistant Editor**
Leslie Huber, M.A.

**Editorial Director**
Dona Herweck Rice

**Editor-in-Chief**
Sharon Coan, M.S.Ed.

**Editorial Manager**
Gisela Lee, M.A.

**Creative Director**
Lee Aucoin

**Illustration Manager/Designer**
Timothy J. Bradley

**Cover Art and Illustration**
Karen Lowe

**Publisher**
Rachelle Cracchiolo, M.S.Ed.

**Teacher Created Materials**
*5301 Oceanus Drive*
*Huntington Beach, CA 92649-1030*
**http://www.tcmpub.com**

**ISBN 978-1-4333-0997-7**

# Annie Oakley

## Story Summary

Born with the name Phoebe Ann Mosey in 1860 to a poor family in Ohio, Annie Oakley struggled to survive. But she learned as a child that she had a talent for shooting a gun. She was so good at it that she hunted small game to help support her family. By the time she was a teenager, those talents took her center stage. As Annie Oakley, she began to amaze audiences all over the world. At a time when women were fighting for basic rights, Annie Oakley became a Western folk hero, an American legend, and an inspiration to women everywhere.

# Tips for Performing Reader's Theater

## Adapted from Aaron Shepard

- Don't let your script hide your face. If you can't see the audience, your script is too high.
- Look up often when you speak. Don't just look at your script.
- Talk slowly so the audience knows what you are saying.
- Talk loudly so everyone can hear you.
- Talk with feelings. If the character is sad, let your voice be sad. If the character is surprised, let your voice be surprised.
- Stand up straight. Keep your hands and feet still.
- Remember that even when you are not talking, you are still your character.
- Narrator, be sure to give the characters enough time for their lines.

# Tips for Performing Reader's Theater *(cont.)*

- If the audience laughs, wait for them to stop before you speak again.
- If someone in the audience talks, don't pay attention.
- If someone walks into the room, don't pay attention.
- If you make a mistake, pretend it was right.
- If you drop something, try to leave it where it is until the audience is looking somewhere else.
- If a reader forgets to read his or her part, see if you can read the part instead, make something up, or just skip over it. Don't whisper to the reader!
- If a reader falls down during the performance, pretend it didn't happen.

# Annie Oakley

## Characters

Narrator
Annie Oakley
Susan Mosey
Frank Butler
Buffalo Bill Cody
Chief Sitting Bull

## Setting

**This reader's theater begins in rural Ohio in 1868. The home of Susan Mosey sits alone at the end of a dirt road. The air is turning cold as autumn nears.**

# Act I

**Narrator:** As Susan Mosey's seven children play outside, she is faced with a big problem. She is worried about how she will feed them this winter, and she wonders if she will lose the farm to the bank. The children's father had been a war hero, but he had become sick and died two years earlier. Susan Mosey remarried and had another baby, but her second husband died, too. Now she isn't sure what she will do.

**Susan:** Children, stop that commotion! Phoebe Ann, come in the house, please. I need to talk to you about something important.

**Annie:** What is it, Mama?

**Susan:** This is the hardest thing I've ever had to say to one of my children. But I simply don't know how I'm going to be able to feed you all this winter. So, I've made arrangements for you to live for a while with the family that runs the county hospital. I'll miss you, Annie, but I know you'll be well taken care of.

**Annie:** But, Mama, I don't want to go. I want to stay here with you!

**Susan:** It's going to be all right, honey. I know you're not the oldest, but I'm asking you to go because you are the most independent. Even at eight years old, you'll be best able to take care of yourself without me around. I know you're going to be just fine.

**Annie:** I'll do whatever you think is best, Mama. Just promise me that you'll come visit and that I'll be able to come home one day.

**Susan:** You have my promise, Annie. Now, go pack your bags. The hospital superintendent and his wife will be picking you up tonight.

**Annie:** All right, Mama.

## Act 2

**Narrator:** At first, Annie is unhappy staying with the hospital superintendent's family. She spends a lot of time working at the hospital and doesn't get to go to school. But she becomes close with the superintendent's wife, who teaches Annie how to cook and sew. Annie's mother visits her often, too. Annie knows she must stay as long as it takes for her family to get back on its feet. One day, on Annie's twelfth birthday, her mother comes to visit.

**Susan:** Annie, it is so wonderful to see you! You are turning into such a fine young woman!

**Annie:** It's good to see you, too, Mama! Do you like this dress I made? I sewed two new dresses for myself this week, and I've made clothes for the rest of the superintendent's children! Maybe one day, I will become a seamstress.

**Susan:** My dear, I have tremendous faith that you will accomplish whatever you set your heart on. Things are changing for women. One day, we may even have the same rights as men! Annie, do you want to see the gift I brought you?

**Annie:** A gift?

**Susan:** You don't think I forgot your birthday, do you? I brought you something very special: your father's hunting rifle.

**Annie:** Papa's gun? But Mama, I've never fired a gun before. I was only six when he died, but I remember watching him shoot. He sure was good at it.

**Susan:** You're a lot like your daddy, Annie. I'm betting you'll be good at it, too. Maybe when you come home, you'll be skilled enough to do some hunting and put some food on the table.

**Annie:** I'll try, Mama!

**Susan:** Come on, honey. Let's go outside and see what you can do. See that tin can across the road? Let's see how close you can come to hitting it.

**Narrator:** Annie's mother shows her how to load the gun. Annie holds it up, steadies it, and fires. She hits the can on the first try!

**Susan:** Goodness! How on earth did you do that, Annie? Are you sure you haven't been taking shooting lessons from the superintendent?

**Annie:** I guess it was just beginner's luck.

**Susan:** We'll see about that. See the branch hanging down from that tree? Let's see if you can hit that.

**Annie:** Oh, Mama, that little branch? I'll never be able to hit that.

**Narrator:** Annie holds the gun up, fires, and shoots the branch right off the tree!

**Annie:** Wow! Maybe it's not beginner's luck, after all!

# Act 3

**Narrator:** For the next few months, all Annie did was practice her shooting. She started with tin cans on a fence. Before long, she was bringing home quail she hunted for dinner. Soon after, Annie returned home to her family. Not only was she able to feed her family with the game she hunted, but she was also able to earn money selling food to the people in town.

## Song: A-Hunting We Will Go

**Narrator:** By the time she was 15, Annie had made enough money to pay for her family's farm. Everyone in town knew of Annie's shooting abilities. When she was just 16, Annie was invited to a shooting competition that featured a famous traveling marksman named Frank Butler.

**Annie:** Mama, look at all the people here. And I'm the only girl! I hope you don't expect me to win. Maybe I should have listened to my brothers. They told me I'd never have a chance competing against grown men.

**Susan:** Just do your best, Annie. Don't listen to what your brothers say. People say they've never seen someone shoot the way you can.

**Annie:** Who is that handsome man over there, Mama? Do you think that's Frank Butler? I've heard that he's the best marksman there is! Oh, he's coming this way!

**Frank:** How do you do, ladies? Let me introduce myself. I am Frank Butler. And I understand this little lady here is quite a brilliant shot. I look forward to our little competition today.

**Annie:** How do you do, Mr. Butler? I look forward to it, as well.

**Narrator:** Annie surprises the audience, shooting all 25 targets. Frank Butler misses one. Annie is declared the winner!

**Frank:** I must admit, Mrs. Mosey, I am most impressed with your daughter's abilities. I'd wager you aren't more than five feet tall, are you, Miss Mosey? Just amazing. You must let me take you both out for supper this evening.

**Narrator:** Annie and her mother accept. And Frank Butler and Annie Mosey wind up falling in love! Some time later, they get married.

## Act 4

**Narrator:** As a married couple, the Butlers traveled together as Frank performed shows with his longtime partner. Annie would help sometimes by holding objects for her husband to shoot. He dazzled the crowds. But on May 1, 1882, Butler's shooting partner was too ill to go on stage.

**Frank:** Annie, we'll have to cancel the show. These people want to be entertained. They don't want to see me come out alone.

**Annie:** How about if I fill in, Frank? It will be fun!

**Frank:** Annie, we both know you're the best shot around—better than me, I admit—but I don't reckon most people are ready to see a woman pulling the trigger of a gun.

**Annie:** Times are changing, Frank. Let's give it a try and see what happens.

**Frank:** They may be changing all right, but we'd better be ready to give them their money back when they see a woman come out. They'll start booing.

**Annie:** I'm going to put on one of my best costumes, Frank. You'll see—people don't care if they're watching a man or a woman. They just want to see some fine shooting!

**Narrator:** Annie amazed the audience with her sharp shooting that day and wound up being a regular part of the act. She changed her stage name from Annie Mosey to Annie Oakley, the name of the town in Ohio where she was born. One day, Buffalo Bill Cody was in the audience. He ran a famous Wild West show and was looking for a new act.

**Buffalo Bill:** Hey, little lady. I just watched your show out there and I'm mighty impressed.

**Annie:** That's high praise coming from you, Mr. Cody.

**Buffalo Bill:** I'm looking for a new act for my show, and I'm wondering if you might like to join me.

**Annie:** What an honor that would be!

**Buffalo Bill:** Let me ask you this: See that man with the brown hat on? Can you shoot the ashes off his cigar?

**Annie:** That man clear across the arena? Well, since there's no one else around . . .

**Narrator:** Annie holds up her rifle and fires. She knocks the ashes right off his cigar.

**Buffalo Bill:** Amazing! That's the best sharpshootin' I've ever seen. Little lady, you're hired!

**Annie:** Wait a minute. Would my husband also be in the show?

**Buffalo Bill:** Well, I don't know. We're really looking for a star attraction.

**Frank:** Annie, Mr. Cody doesn't need me in his show. But what you need, Annie, is someone to manage your act. And that's where I come in. Yes, Mr. Cody, my wife is interested in joining your show. Now, let's talk business.

**Annie:** Frank, are you sure?

**Frank:** Annie, you've always been a better shot than I am. I'm ready to leave the stage and make sure your talents are seen all over the world.

**Narrator:** Beginning in 1885 and for the next 17 years, Annie was the star attraction of Buffalo Bill's Wild West show, amazing audiences worldwide.

## Act 5

**Buffalo Bill:** Annie, I've got some big news. We're beginning a tour of Europe next week, and you're going to be performing for the queen of England!

**Annie:** Queen Victoria? Why would she be interested in a girl who shoots guns?

**Buffalo Bill:** Annie, don't sell yourself short. This summer alone, almost half a million people came to the show just to see you.

**Annie:** Hard to believe that so many people pay money to see a gal shoot an apple off someone's head!

**Buffalo Bill:** You do a lot more than that, Annie. Who else could shoot the flame off a candle with a .22 rifle? Who else could shoot a dime tossed in midair—from 90 feet? Who else could shoot 4,500 out of 5,000 glass balls tossed in midair like you did in the last show? People can't believe it until they see it with their own two eyes!

**Annie:** Well, performing for the queen is going to be quite an honor.

**Buffalo Bill:** And don't forget about tonight's show. Chief Sitting Bull will be there.

**Annie:** Chief Sitting Bull? The leader of the Lakota warriors?

**Buffalo Bill:** Yup, he's the one who beat General Custer's force in the battle of Little Bighorn. I think he may be joining our show.

**Narrator:** After that evening's show, Chief Sitting Bull approaches Annie.

**Sitting Bull:** I am most impressed with your talents, Miss Oakley.

**Annie:** Why thank you, Chief.

**Sitting Bull:** If I might say so, I like that you don't see the need to wear fancy costumes or put paint on your face like so many other women your age.

**Annie:** You mean makeup? I don't have patience for it. It seems so foolish. I am here not so people can judge me on my looks, but so that they can appreciate what I can do with a gun.

**Sitting Bull:** You remind me of my own daughter. But she is gone now. I miss her very much.

**Annie:** I am sorry, Chief. I take it as a great compliment that I remind you of her. Could she shoot, too?

| | |
|---|---|
| **Sitting Bull:** | Oh, no. But she was good with a bow and arrow! It is my hope that the two of us can be friends. I will call you Little Sure Shot. |
| **Annie:** | Little Sure Shot? I like that, Chief! I hope it's true what I hear about you joining Buffalo Bill's show. I would like to get to know you better. |
| **Sitting Bull:** | I am not sure about joining your troupe. I know that there are those who don't trust my people. |
| **Annie:** | I promise you that you will enjoy your time with the show. And you will be able to teach everyone a thing or two about your people. |
| **Sitting Bull:** | I would be able to bring home many stories, I am sure. It is my hope that you and I can learn much from each other. Maybe you can teach me how to fire a gun, and I can show you how to use a bow and arrow. Although, I will bet that your aim with both is better than mine! |

**Narrator:** Sitting Bull and Annie became good friends, and he eventually adopted her as his daughter. Annie went on to become America's first female superstar. Many women took up the sport of shooting because of her. Annie and Frank gave away most of their money to charities and lived a long, happy life together. Annie Oakley became an American legend and an inspiration to women all over the world.

**Poem: Don't Quit**

# Don't Quit

## Credited to Edgar Guest

When things go wrong, as they sometimes will,
When the road you're trudging seems all uphill,
When the funds are low and the debts are high,
And you want to smile but you have to sigh,
When care is pressing you down a bit,
Rest if you must, but do not quit.

Life is strange with its twists and turns,
As everyone of us sometimes learns.
And many a fellow turns about
When he might have won had he stuck it out.
Don't give up though the pace seems slow—
You may succeed with another blow.

Success is failure turned inside out—
The silver tint of the clouds of doubt.
And you never can tell how close you are,
It may be near when it seems afar.
So stick to the fight when you're hardest hit—
It's when things seem worst you must not quit.

# A-Hunting We Will Go

## Traditional

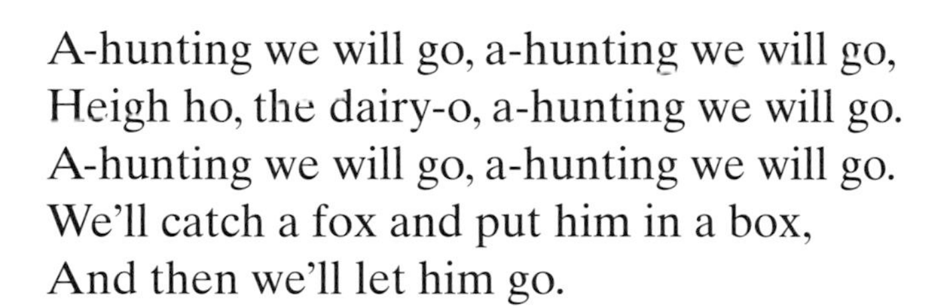

A-hunting we will go, a-hunting we will go,
Heigh ho, the dairy-o, a-hunting we will go.
A-hunting we will go, a-hunting we will go.
We'll catch a fox and put him in a box,
And then we'll let him go.

A-hunting we will go, a-hunting we will go,
Heigh ho, the dairy-o, a-hunting we will go.
A-hunting we will go, a-hunting we will go.
We'll catch a fish and put him on a dish,
And then we'll let him go.

A-hunting we will go, a-hunting we will go,
Heigh ho, the dairy-o, a-hunting we will go.
A-hunting we will go, a-hunting we will go.
We'll catch a bear and cut his hair,
And then we'll let him go.

A-hunting we will go, a-hunting we will go,
Heigh ho, the dairy-o, a-hunting we will go.
A-hunting we will go, a-hunting we will go.
We'll catch a pig and dance a little jig,
And then we'll let him go.

# Glossary

**arrangements**—things prepared and put into order

**brilliant**—unusually good

**commotion**—noisy disturbance

**game**—wild animals hunted for food

**independent**—not relying on another or others for aid or support

**marksman**—someone skilled at shooting guns

**reckon**—to think about; consider

**rural**—relating to the country

**superintendent**—a person who is in charge of an organization

**troupe**—a group of performers

**trudging**—walking or marching, usually with difficulty